For Jennifer

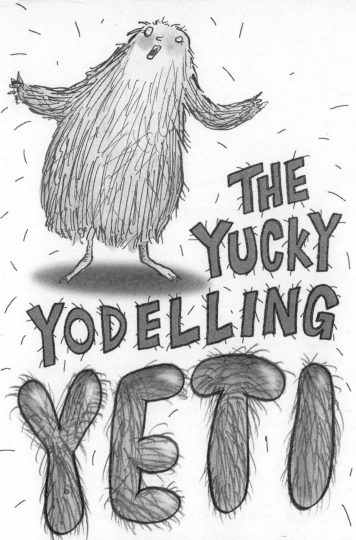

THE YUCKY YODELLING YETI

GILLIAN JOHNSON

A Catalogue record for this book is available
from the British Library

ISBN: 978 1 444 90357 7

Typeset and designed by Fiona Webb

Printed and bound by
CPI Group (UK) Ltd, Croydon, CR0 4YY

The paper and board used in this paperback by
Hodder Children's Books are natural recyclable products
made from wood grown in sustainable forests. The manufacturing
processes conform to the environmental regulations of
the country of origin.

Hodder Children's Books
a division of Hachette Children's Books
338 Euston Road, London NW1 3BH
An Hachette UK company
www.hachette.co.uk

It was Christmas Eve at

MONSTER HOSPITAL.

But the four doctors were having a hard time sleeping ...

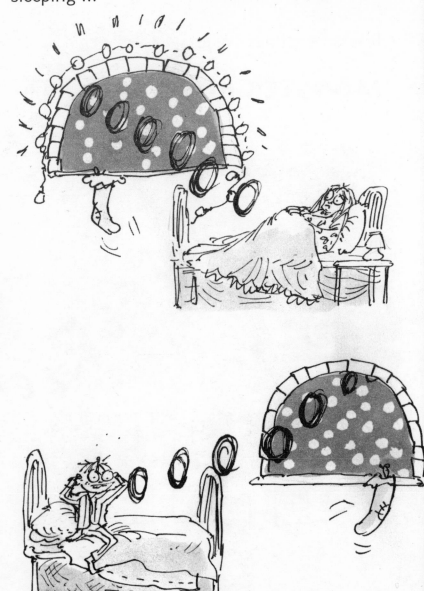

... because something outside was screeching and screaming.

Only Tom could think straight. He dashed through the corridor to the decibel-o-meter.

The needle registered 100 decibels. In other words, loud enough to cause damage to a human being's ears.

He sounded the alarm.

There is a creature in trouble! If it can't come to us, then we have to go to it!

'EMERGENCY! EMERGENCY!

There's a monster out there who needs our help!'

Carolyn, Sylvie and Dylan got out of bed and came to find Tom. But they were not happy. Who could blame them?

These children would never even have
spoken to each other if they hadn't had
snuffly colds ...

... been shoved into quarantine ...

... and climbed through the medicine cabinet into another world, where Sister Winifred put them to work at **MONSTER HOSPITAL**.

Yes, they were a team.

A team of doctors taking care of sick and injured monsters.

But that didn't make them friends ...

9

click click click

It was Sister Winifred!

'Tom is right!' she said. 'It takes a monster to find a monster.

'As I have said before, *that makes you four
more than qualified!*'

She pulled up a large trunk filled with winter
clothes. 'Hurry up! No time to waste!'

Bundled up, they ventured out into the freezing dark.

And **HOWLING** wind.
And waist-deep **SNOW**.

'This is the worst night of my life,'
complained Sylvie bitterly.
    Nobody could hear her.

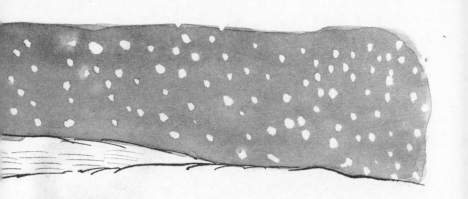

Leading the way, Tom noticed something weird in the snow. He picked it up. 'Look at this!' he cried. But then his torch lit up something else.

A **GIANT** footprint!

And another ...

... and another two!

The footsteps stopped in front
of a huge snowdrift. Dylan
pushed ahead, ready to climb it.

Suddenly the snowdrift

SHOOK.

19

'What is it?' whispered Tom.

'Uhm ... a snowman?' mumbled Dylan.

'A polar bear?' wondered Sylvie.

'A ... sasquatch?' gasped Carolyn.

EEEEK

Holding its paws to its ears, whatever it was
turned to run away ...

... but its legs wobbled and it slumped on its bum.

'Wait a minute!' cried Tom, remembering his facts. **It's a YETI!**

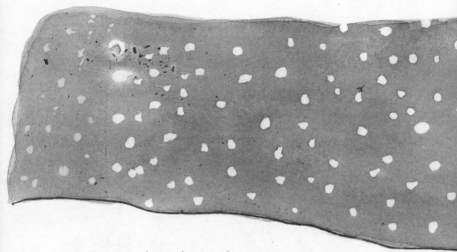

'A large white hairy beast resembling a bear and said to live in the Himalayas!' added Tom.

'What is it doing *here*?' demanded Sylvie.
'A very good question!' replied Tom.

While they were talking, the creature
started to roll away.

'Where are you going?' shouted Tom.

'AWWWWWW,'
hollered the yeti.

They watched,
helpless. **How could
they stop it?**

27

They all had the same idea. They lined
up and started to roll the yeti back in the

direction of the hospital, which was quite
easy because it was downhill.

And, as they rolled, something miraculous
began to happen.

The yeti's voice grew smaller and smaller
and its body grew **BIGGER**

AND

BIGGER ...

AND

BIGGER

just the way a snowball grows when you
roll it to make a snowman.

Finally, they reached
the castle:

34

HEAVE HO

through the front door ...

... and **HEAVE HO** into the Quiet Room.

There was total silence, except for ...

Sister Winifred!

'Has your patient been caught in
an avalanche?' she asked.
'It's a yeti!' announced Carolyn.

'It was making that terrible noise,'
added Dylan.

'Hmmmm,' said Sister Winifred.

From deep within the
snow came a muffled noise.

'HPPPPP MMMMMMMEEEEE!!!!!'

'Don't you have to be able to HEAR your patient?' asked Sister Winifred.

'Yes,' said Dylan. 'Except that the noise it makes is **terrible!**'

'So,' said Sister Winifred, 'you are not the little monsters I thought you were ...'

'YES WE ARE!'

She handed out four shovels. 'Then get cracking!'

The snow had hardened around the yeti's body.

'It's like concrete!' puffed Dylan.

At one end, two feet popped out.
Sylvie checked them for frostbite.

The doctors shovelled and chipped and finally smashed their way through the ice and snow, uncovering:

a small brown nose,
two glittery black eyes,
and some teeth.

And something else.

They all backed away.
'**HALITOSIS!**' spluttered Sylvie.
'Hali-what?' asked Carolyn.

'Halitosis means *bad breath*,'
explained Tom, backing away.

At a safe distance,
they changed into
their lab coats.

Suddenly there was a groan ...

The yeti stood up.
It was a scary sight!

49

But no sooner had it risen than it fell, clutching its head and moaning.

'I think it's his ears!' said Carolyn.
The yeti nodded.

'Otitis media,' said Tom.

'A simple earache?' snorted Sylvie. 'That's not serious.'

Tom would never forget the horrible earaches he had when he was small. 'Earaches are not only extremely painful,' he said. 'They can make you deaf!'

Sylvie apologised and turned back to the yeti. 'What's *your name?*' she asked loudly.

No reply.

It was time to find the right medicine.

Sylvie squeezed three drops in each yeti ear.
The yeti groaned and muttered something.

'*Who* will marry someone else?'
said Carolyn.

Tom stood close. 'Can you
please explain?'

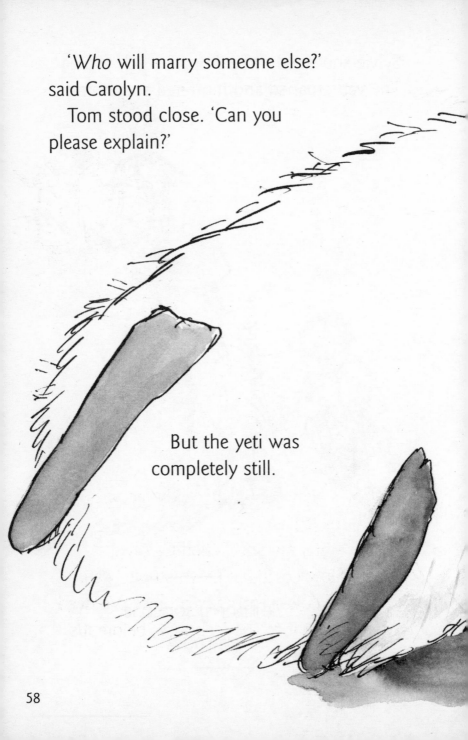

But the yeti was
completely still.

'Hey,' said Dylan. 'My feet are soaked.'

'It's melting!' cried Carolyn. 'How could we be so stupid? Yetis are cold-weather creatures! We need to get it to the icehouse, before it's too late!'

The children lined up
and rolled the melting yeti
through the corridor,

... down
   down
      down the crumbly steps ...

... to the **ICEHOUSE**, a cold storage room in the basement. It was used for things they could not fit in the fridge: frozen chickens, ice cream, and now a melting yeti with otitis media.

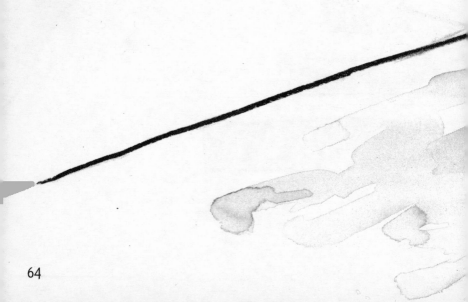

In the icy cold air, the yeti tried to stand up.
The noise it made was bad.

But the **SMELL OF ITS BREATH** was worse!
The children ran out, slamming the door.

'How long does it take for the medicine to start working?' asked Carolyn.

'It says ten minutes on the bottle,' said Sylvie.

'What about medicine for bad breath?' asked Dylan.

'Like some anti-volatile-sulphur spray,' said Tom.

'No, it just needs to brush its teeth,' said Sylvie.

'And its tongue,' said Dylan.

'Bad breath comes from anaerobic bacteria letting off farts in the mouth,' said Tom.

'Let's review our notes,' ordered Sylvie.

1. Name _____ ?
2. Age _____ ?
3. MONSTER TYPE _____ Ye
4. DWELLING _____ otitis
5. WHAT'S WRONG? ↘ _____
6. What else? makes
7. What else? _____
8. More? will
9. MEDICINE SEVERE
10. Misc. ear drops

71

'Dwelling?' asked Sylvie.

Tom spoke. 'I have heard about two yeti tribes in the Super North Mountains.'

'Where?' asked Sylvie.

'Super north of here,' said Tom.

She wrote it down. 'Anything else?'

'Yes,' said Tom. 'Remember just before the yeti passed out? It said something very weird.'

'Yes,' cried Sylvie. 'It said, "He'll marry someone else".'

'**YUCK!**' said Dylan.

'When the yeti wakes, we'll ask it about that,' said Sylvie. 'Now what about that thing you found in the snow?'

'You mean this?' asked Tom.

'Cool!' said Dylan.

'What is it?' asked Sylvie.

'It looks like a French Horn!' said Carolyn.

Tom tried to blow.

'You just don't know how to use it,' said Dylan, giving it a go.

Then Carolyn grabbed it.

'My turn,' said Sylvie. 'Maybe it's blocked with snow.'

She turned it upside down, put the mouthpiece in her ear and pressed the other end against the icehouse wall.

'It's awake!'
she announced.
'It sounds MUCH calmer.
We need to go in there and speak to it.'

'Then it can go home!' said Dylan, wanting
to get on with Christmas.

'I don't think it's that simple,' Tom said.
'Hasn't anyone wondered why a yeti would
get an earache in the first place? Yetis LIVE in
snow, blizzards and wind. Something doesn't
add up. Come on, we really need to talk to
our patient.'

'No way,' said Dylan. 'Not me.'

'I'm going to go and look for some monster mouthwash,' he said.

'Come on, Tom, we're going to the icehouse,' called Carolyn.

When the yeti saw the doctors it scrambled
to its feet, grinding its yellow teeth.

Tom held up the object. 'Is this yours?'

'**My engagement ear trumpet!**'
said the yeti.

The children were confused.
'*Engagement?*'
'*Ear trumpet?*'

'It was outside – on the ground,' said Tom.

'Not far from where we found *you*,' said Sylvie.

'Yelling your head off,' added Carolyn.

The yeti looked indignant. 'I *never* yell my head off. I only yodel.'

The doctors wondered whether they had heard correctly. **Yodel?**

'My grandmother yodels,' Tom remembered fondly.

Sylvie elbowed him. 'Shush!'

One by one the yeti looked at them. 'Who are **you**?' it asked.

'My ears?' said the yeti. 'My ears did hurt but are fine now. Where am I?'

'But I'll miss my wedding if I stay here,' said the yeti. 'Oh Yan, *where are you?*'

The yeti stuck the skinny part of the trumpet in its ear ...

'That hurt soooo much!' whimpered the yeti. 'My ear is still sore.'

'Otitis media usually takes a few days to heal completely,' said Tom.

'Who is Yan?' asked Carolyn.

My *fiancé*. I need to hear Yan's yodel.

'What is Yan's yodel?' asked Sylvie.

'It's a wedding custom,' said the yeti, forgetting the pain for a moment. 'The bride spends the night before the wedding in her parents' igloo, while the groom spends the night in the new marriage igloo.

In the morning, the groom yodels to his fiancée. She follows his song, finds her new igloo and the wedding is held there. Get it?'

'That is *soooo romantic*,' said Carolyn. 'Are you the bride or the groom?'

The yeti stared in horror at Carolyn. 'It's pretty obvious, isn't it? I have long eyelashes!'

'Sorry,' said Carolyn.

'You still haven't told us your name,'
said Sylvie.

'Yuki.'

'Yuki means **SNOW** in Japanese!' said Tom.

Yuki snuffled. 'Yuki means ME. And I'm the
bride! Or I was supposed to be the bride ...
until the blizzard got into my ears ... and my
head ... and ruined everything!'

'What do you mean, the blizzard got into your ears?' asked Tom.

'Yan's song sounded all *fizzy*,' continued Yuki. 'I couldn't follow it. I couldn't find him. **Now he'll marry someone else.**'

Very upset, Yuki took a deep breath. An all-too-familiar noise welled up in her chest.

'**Quick!**' cried Sylvie.

'**Run!**' yelled Carolyn.

The cry was loud. But not **too** terrible.

Tom knew Yuki's ears hurt too much to hear her fiancé. But he could help.

'We need to find Yan,' he announced. 'Who's coming with me?'

'Not me,' said Dylan.

'No way,' said Carolyn.

Tom held up the ear trumpet. 'This is going to take me to Yan.'

'To take **us**,' said Sylvie. 'I'm coming with you.'

Tom reminded Carolyn and Dylan to keep an eye on Yuki. Sylvie passed them the ear drops.

'Come on Sylvie, we have to move fast!' said Tom.

Up the crumbly steps ...

... into the winter clothes ...

... and out into the dark night, on old skis
from Sister Winifred's trunk.

Sylvie looked at the snow. 'Yuki's fiancé could be anywhere!'

'The ear trumpet will help us find Yan,' said Tom. 'It works like a hearing aid, collecting sound waves and making them louder.

If Yan is out here, we'll hear him.'

'This is a good place,' said Tom.
He put the trumpet into his ear and listened carefully.

But things did not go according to plan.
An icy gust blew snow into the trumpet.

'Now I know why Yuki has an earache!' cried Tom. 'The ear trumpet funnels the snow right into your eardrum. It really is like having a blizzard in your ear! Now I know what—'

But the skis seemed to have a mind of their own. 'Hold on!' Sylvie cried.

They **WHOOSHED** down the hill.
Across a frozen pond.
Through a path in the woods ...

... to the edge of a pine forest.

'Yan?' shouted Tom.

The trees seemed to be moving in time to a mysterious song. Once again, Tom thought of his grandmother who yodelled to her goats.

But it wasn't Tom's grandmother who lurched towards them. It was another yeti, with shaggy fur and blazing eyes.

It glared at Tom and Sylvie.

It glared at the ear trumpet.

It **GROWLED**.

'MY ENGAGEMENT EAR TRUMPET!'

it cried. 'What have you done with my
fiancée? Where is Yuki?'

'She's at M-M-Monster Hospital,'
stammered Sylvie.

'With otitis m-m-media,' stuttered Tom.

'And bad halitosis,' added Sylvie.

The yeti's eyes narrowed. 'Otis? Bad Hal?'

'Yes,' nodded Sylvie. 'It was quite serious ...'

'Quite serious, you say? You mean she
loves others and not me? She loves Otis
and Bad Hal?

SHE'S DUMPED ME, HASN'T SHE?'

113

Tom and Sylvie could hardly breathe. This yeti's breath was even worse than Yuki's!

'She didn't dump you!' gagged Tom. 'There are no other fellows! Otitis media is not another yeti. It's an earache.'

'And halitosis is a medical condition. It means bad breath,' added Sylvie.

'It's Yan she loves. You *are* Yan, aren't you?' asked Tom.

'Yep,' said Yan.

'Yuki used the ear trumpet to find you,' said Sylvie, 'but the icy air blew into her ears and made them too sore to hear your yodel.'

'Poor Yuki!' said Yan. 'No Otis? No Bad Hal? That's a big relief. Please point the way to my Yuki, doctors!'

The doctors couldn't keep up with Yan's giant steps, so he lifted them and strode down the snowy hill, back through the woods ...

... across the pond ...

... to **MONSTER HOSPITAL** ...

... where they found
Yuki eating ice cream
in the icehouse.

Yuki looked at Yan.
Yan looked at Yuki.

Yan broke out into the most triumphant
yodel anyone had ever heard.

In response, Yuki took a deep breath.

HER BODY SHIVERED.

HER NOSTRILS **QUIVERED**.

HER TEETH GLITTERED.

Then she threw back her head and yodelled
as if her life depended on it.
And to the children's astonishment ...

It was beautiful.

'*YOU DIDN'T DUMP ME!*' cried Yan.

'No,' said Yuki.

'I have been yodelling far and wide for you, Yuki.'

'I've been listening far and wide for you, Yan!'

Yan looked at the doctors.
'We have to get to our wedding!'
he announced. 'The herd is waiting.'
'You can go if you promise to take your
medicine,' said Tom.
'And stay out of the wind with
your ear trumpet,' said Sylvie.
'Yes, I promise!' Yuki held up
the ear medicine. 'I heard
what you said. Three
drops, three times a day.'

But how did Yuki's terrible noise turn into music?

Love is the best medicine!

'It didn't help their halitosis,' said Dylan, offering up a bag of goodies. 'Wedding presents! Mouthwash, floss ...'

'No thanks,' the yetis chorused. For Yan and
Yuki liked the smell of each other's yeti breath.

And before you could say *halitosis*, Yan
took Yuki by the paw ...

... and together they trundled off, out of **MONSTER HOSPITAL** in the direction of the Super Far North, where yetis get married and live happily ever after.

It was Sister Winifred with some
Christmas puddings and presents.

When the presents were opened, Sister Winifred smiled broadly. 'Now, I am sure that all of you are in a rush to get back to school ...'

NO WE'RE NOT!

'Oh, you **are** the little monsters that I thought you were!' sang Sister Winifred.

‘Yo-lady-oh!’

**Hodder
Children's
Books**

Turn the page

for more fantastic fiction

from Hodder Children's Books ...

Stone Goblins

Tree Goblin

Puddle Goblin

GOBLINS

By David Melling

Shadow Goblin

Ghost Goblin